WALKER CLASSICS

The DUCK in the GUN

WRITTEN BY
JOY COWLEY

ILLUSTRATED BY
ROBYN BELTON

WALKER BOOKS
AND SUBSIDIARIES

LONDON • BOSTON • SYDNEY • AUCKLAND

For days, the General and his men had been marching. Now they were at the town and ready for war.

The General called his Gunner. "Is the gun in place?"

"Yes, Sir," the Gunner replied.

"Is it aimed at the town?"

"It is, Sir," said the Gunner.

"Good," said the General. "Load it. When I give the order, fire."

"Understood, Sir," said the Gunner, and he went away.

Moments later, the Gunner came back. "Sir! We can't fire the gun."

"Why not?" snapped the General.

"Because we can't load it, Sir."

The General grew red in the face. "Why can't you load it?"

"Please, Sir," said the Gunner. "There's a duck in the gun."

"A duck?" cried the General. "You mean a–"

"Yes, Sir. It goes quack-quack! Sir, it has made a nest in the gun."

"The cheek of it!" shouted the General. "Get rid of it at once!"

"I've tried," said the Gunner, "but it won't come out. I think it's sitting on some eggs."

"I'll soon fix that," said the General, picking up his sword. "A duck can't stop an army."

The General and the Gunner went out to where the gun had been set, aimed at the town.

The General looked down the gun and saw two small eyes looking back at him. "Here, dilly, dilly, dilly," he called. "Nice dilly."

The duck quacked but didn't move.

The General became angry. "Come out, blast you!" he bellowed, banging on the gun with his sword.

There was another quack, but the duck did not stir from her nest.

The General paced up and down. "I can't have a duck upsetting my plans!"
he muttered.

"There is something you could do, Sir," said one of the men. "You could fire
the gun with the duck inside."

"No, no, no!" said the General. "We'll think of something else. Ah! I know,
we'll borrow a gun."

The General put on all his medals, polished his boots and, with a white flag in his hand, went to the town.

"Take me to your Prime Minister," he said to the town guards.

The guards led him through the streets to the Prime Minister's house. When the General knocked, the door was opened by the Prime Minister's daughter.

"Good afternoon," said the General. "Do you know who I am?"

"Oh, yes," said the young woman. "I've seen your picture in the paper. Won't you come in?" She turned and called, "Father, here is the General to see you."

The Prime Minister appeared. "How do you do, General?"

"Not very well," he sighed. Then he told the Prime Minister about the duck in the gun.

"What are you going to do about it?" asked the Prime Minister.

The General coughed and looked at the floor. "That's why I came to see you. I was wondering if you could lend us a gun. It's not a very fair war if you have guns and we haven't."

"Oh, I agree," said the Prime Minister. "But you see, we have only one gun."

"Couldn't we share it?" asked the General. "You could fire a shot at us, then we could take the gun and fire a shot at you."

The Prime Minister laughed. "Goodness, no! That would never do! Besides, our gun is far too heavy to move."

The General's moustache drooped.

"The answer is clear," said the Prime Minister. "You'll have to put the war off for three weeks. By that time, the duck will have hatched her eggs, and you will have your gun back."

The two men shook hands.

"Fair enough," said the General. "We'll forget about the war for three weeks."

When the soldiers heard the news, they were very pleased. Three weeks holiday! They were so delighted they put food down the gun when the General wasn't looking.

But after one week, the General had another problem. He put on his medals, picked up the white flag and, once more, went to see the Prime Minister.

"How are you?" asked the Prime Minister.

"Not good at all," said the General. "The truth is, I'm running out of money. For a whole week my men have done nothing, and they expect to be paid for it."

"That is a problem," said the Prime Minister.

"I don't suppose you could lend me some money," said the General.

"No," said the Prime Minister. "Men should not get money for doing nothing. However, I can pay your soldiers if they will work for me. See our town? It needs painting. The houses are shabby and the shops look a mess. In two weeks your men could paint the whole town."

"What a great idea!" said the General. "Thanks very much. I'll tell my men at once."

This time, the men were not so pleased. But when the General said he could no longer pay them, they agreed to work in the town.

Early next morning, they put on old clothes and left the camp.

The General went out to look at the gun. The duck was still there, sitting on her nest and quacking to herself. The General looked over his shoulder to make sure he was alone. He took some cake from his pocket and quickly put it down the gun, then he spent the rest of the morning sitting in the sun, reading.

Every day, the men went to work in the town. The camp was very quiet.
Sometimes, the General would look at the town through his spyglass, and
watch it change colour.

Sometimes, he visited the Prime Minister and his daughter and drank tea
in their garden.

Sometimes, he just walked as far as the gun, with a pocket full of bread
or biscuits.

Near the end of the third week, the eggs hatched.

The General walked past the gun. He heard not only *quack-quack-quack*, but also a tiny *beep-beep-beep*. He rang the alarm bell as loudly as he could.

At once, the men put down their paint and brushes and ran back to camp.

"Attention!" called the General. "The duck's eggs have hatched." He looked inside the gun. "Here, dilly, dilly."

Out popped a little head. It was the first duckling.

Very carefully, the General lifted it to the ground.

Then another duckling came out, and another, until there were eight baby ducks waddling around the General's feet.

Last out was the mother duck. She looked at all the men and quacked loudly. Then she flew down to her ducklings and marched them off across the grass.

"Three cheers for the duck," shouted the men, throwing their hats in the air.

"Hooray, hooray, hooray!"

"Now we can use our gun again," said the General. "Now we can have a war."

The soldiers stopped cheering. They became very quiet. They stood with
their hats in their hands and looked at the ground.

"Please, Sir," said the Gunner. "We can't shoot at that town. We would spoil
the new paint."

"Yes," said one of the men. "We've worked for weeks on those houses."

The General nodded. It did seem silly to blow up freshly painted houses. Besides, he had become rather fond of the Prime Minister's daughter.

"What will we do?" he said.

"You couldn't put the war off for good, could you, Sir?" said the Gunner. "After we've finished painting the town, we can all go home."

The General thought for a long time. "All right," he said. "I'll go and tell the Prime Minister."

So that was the end of the war.

The men finished their painting, and the General married the Prime Minister's daughter. It was a big wedding with flowers, and a cake that had a white sugar gun on top.

Of course, the duck came ...

She and her eight ducklings were there to march behind the army band.

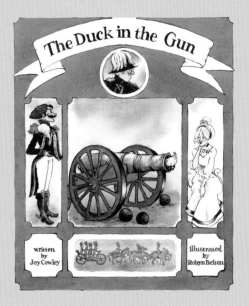

Every so often a book will come into your life that will stay with you for years, its impact going beyond the words and illustrations appearing on the page.

For me, *The Duck in the Gun* has been one of those titles, a book I first read some 21 years ago when I was training to be a primary school teacher.

Published in 1984 by Shortland Educational "for use as a graded reading book in schools", *The Duck in the Gun* was immediately recognised by many teachers and librarians as being so much more than a reader; a rare gem that transcended its format in originality and execution.

When I became a specialist children's bookseller in 1994, *The Duck in the Gun* was one of a few educational titles we stocked in our New Zealand section. By this time I was far more aware of its sheer brilliance – the perfect collaboration between author and illustrator to deliver an important message in a simple story with light humour.

This surely has to be the most inspirational title Joy Cowley and Robyn Belton have published together; its message of the futility of war and the security of peaceful coexistence is as relevant today as it ever was.

It pleases me greatly that, in the year of its 25th anniversary, *The Duck in the Gun*, with its wonderful new format and subtle text changes that give it the significance it deserves, will become readily available to a wider readership. Now it can take its rightful place as a New Zealand classic.

Here's hoping future generations will delight in the hatching of ducklings rather than the fighting of wars.

Julie Harper, Jabberwocky Children's Bookshop

For all those who work for peace in the world,
and for all those who don't.

This edition published in 2009
by Walker Books Australia Pty Ltd
Locked Bag 22, Newtown,
NSW 2042 Australia
www.walkerbooks.com.au

First published by Doubleday and Co., New York, in 1969
Republished by Shortland Educational Publications, New Zealand, in 1984

National Library of Australia Cataloguing-in-Publication entry:

Cowley, Joy, 1936-
The duck in the gun / Joy Cowley ; illustrator, Robyn Belton.

Rev. ed.

Newtown, N.S.W. : Walker Books Australia, 2009.

ISBN: 978 1 921150 83 8 (pbk.)

For children.
War–Juvenile fiction.

Other Authors/Contributors: Belton, Robyn.

NZ823.2

Typeset in Aunt Mildred
Printed and bound in China

2 4 6 8 10 9 7 5 3 1

Stories seldom begin with one idea. More often, two ideas collide, coalesce and form a magnet for other ideas and words. *The Duck in the Gun* started in the late 1960s as intense feelings of distress about the Vietnam War. I felt helpless. How could a writer get an anti-war message to the next generation? The answer came with a small news item about something entirely different. In Chicago, construction was halted for three weeks because a duck had made a nest on a building site. That happy little story flew to my heart and connected with my thoughts about war.

About this time, a small New Zealand publishing company, Price Milburn, advertised a competition for picture books. I submitted *The Duck in the Gun*. It won; but after a year the company decided it could not afford to publish it, and I sent it to Doubleday, New York, who were then publishing my adult novels. *The Duck in the Gun* came out in 1969 with illustrations by Edward Sorel who was better known for his *Playboy* cartoons! It went out of print in the early 1970s and ten years later was revived in New Zealand by Wendy Pye of Shortland Publications, with charming illustrations by Robyn Belton. But a 32 page picture book was an orphan with no logical place in Shortland's early reading programs, and so it too went out of print.

For the last decade, Robyn and I have had countless requests from librarians and teachers for a reprint of *The Duck in the Gun*. We are delighted that Walker Books are bringing it back with Robyn's child-centred pictures. Perhaps the duck will show another generation of children that it's war and not people that is the enemy.

Joy Cowley

JOY COWLEY, one of New Zealand's most celebrated authors, has been writing books for children and adults for 50 years. Her many awards include the AW Reed Award, the Margaret Mahy Lecture Award, an OBE for services to children's literature, and a DCNZM (a Damehood in the old honour system). Her strong patronage of both children's literature and literacy led to the establishment of the Joy Cowley Picture Book Award.

I loved illustrating this story. Right from the start I was drawn into its humour and its compassion. Joy's brief to her illustrator was to set the story somewhere in Europe in the 19th century. I interpreted this place as "Ruritanian", a mythical site for 19th century comic opera.

As you can imagine, I had many field days gathering images. Excursions took me to visit museums and libraries where I found rich images of military fashions. The local Black Powder Club, whose members provided fascinating information about the art of bombardiering, also gave me access to a model of a twelve-pounder cannon. I learned that it took five soldiers to man one cannon and six horses to pull it into battle. I found there was one soldier whose job was to dress the General properly in his finery. On his belt he wore two pouches: one holding polish for the General's boots and the other, wax for his moustache.

In the pictures I have added a dog which is not in Joy's text at all. The dog functions as a "mirror", amplifying the gestures and expressions of the girl.

The Duck in the Gun meant a lot to both Joy and myself as it was Joy's first anti-war book. That this story has a pacifist sentiment makes it as relevant today as when it was first written. Significantly, it has been chosen by the Hiroshima Peace Memorial Museum as one of ten selected children's book titles from around the world.

Robyn Belton

ROBYN BELTON is one of New Zealand's most highly regarded children's book illustrators. Her many awards include the Russell Clark Award, several New Zealand Post Children's Book Awards, and the Margaret Mahy Medal. Robyn also runs workshops throughout New Zealand for both children and adults and her work has been exhibited in New Zealand, Italy and Japan.

Walker Books is proud to be publishing these
classic Australian and New Zealand picture books.

Available from all good bookstores.

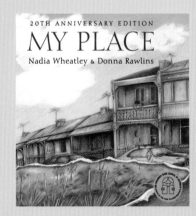